RAPUNZEL

A tale by the Brothers Grimm

retold and illustrated by

J U T T A   A S H

HOLT, RINEHART AND WINSTON
NEW YORK

ONCE upon a time, there lived a man and his wife; the one thing they lacked was a child. Now at the top of their house was a little room with a window which looked out over a beautiful walled garden. In it grew the loveliest flowers and the most luscious fruit and vegetables. But the wall around was high; and, even worse, the garden belonged to a witch!

One day the wife noticed a bed planted with a special kind of fresh green lettuce known as rapunzel. How she longed to taste it! Very soon she could think of nothing else. Day by day she grew paler and thinner, until she had dwindled into a shadow of herself, for no other food could tempt her, nothing at all.

HER husband was alarmed to see her fading away. "Wife, wife," he said. "What is troubling you?" "It's the rapunzel in that garden," she replied. "I shall die unless I have some to eat."

"What's to be done?" thought the good man. "If she must have it, she must, witch or no witch." So, that very evening, he scrambled over the high wall, stealthily pulled up a bunch and brought it back to his wife. Oh, she was overjoyed! She made it into a salad and—crunch, crunch, how delicious!—in a minute there wasn't a shred left. Next day, she craved for that same salad even more; there was nothing else she would eat.

WHAT could her husband do? Again he waited until dusk and climbed into the magic garden. He bent down to pick up a quick handful of the rapunzel, but what a fright awaited him! There, standing over him, was the witch herself, wild with rage. "Thief!" she cried. "You'll regret it!"

"Forgive me," begged the poor man, and he told her of his wife's great longing for the leaves. The witch grew calmer as she listened.

"Very well," she said at last. "You may take as much as you need, but on one condition. As soon as your wife has a child, you must give that child to me. It will be well looked after, I promise you."

WELL, the man was so relieved that the witch had not worked some dreadful spell on him, that he quickly agreed to the bargain. Sure enough, when the wife gave birth to a beautiful baby girl soon afterward, the witch arrived promptly to claim her debt. "Rapunzel shall be her name!" she declared, and she carried the child away.

What a beautiful girl she grew up to be! But when she was twelve years old the witch shut her up in a high tower, far away in a wood. The tower had neither door nor staircase, only a tiny window right at the top. Whenever the witch came to visit her charge, she would call up to the window:

Rapunzel, Rapunzel,
Let down your golden hair!

FOR Rapunzel had wonderful long golden hair which she often wore in thick plaits. Each time she heard the witch's call she would wind the plaits round the hook on the window ledge and let them fall all the way down to the ground. The witch would then seize hold and climb up until she reached the window.

Some years passed, and one day a young prince was riding through the wood. He heard the sound of sweet singing, followed the voice and found himself at the foot of a tall tower. But where was the door? Who was the singer? Whoever it was, the voice was so enchanting that the prince came day after day to listen.

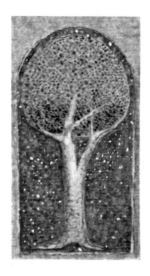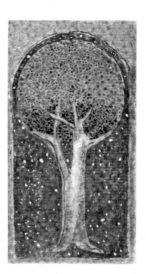

ONE evening, from his hiding place behind a tree, the prince saw a strange woman emerge from the wood and stand at the foot of the tower. There she called out these words:

> *Rapunzel, Rapunzel,*
> *Let down your golden hair!*

At once a great length of golden hair slid to the ground, and the woman hauled herself up to the window.

"Aha!" thought the prince. "A ladder for one is a ladder for another!" So the next evening he too stood at the foot of the tower and called up:

> *Rapunzel, Rapunzel,*
> *Let down your golden hair!*

Immediately the shining hair fell to his feet, and the prince climbed up and up until he reached the window at the top.

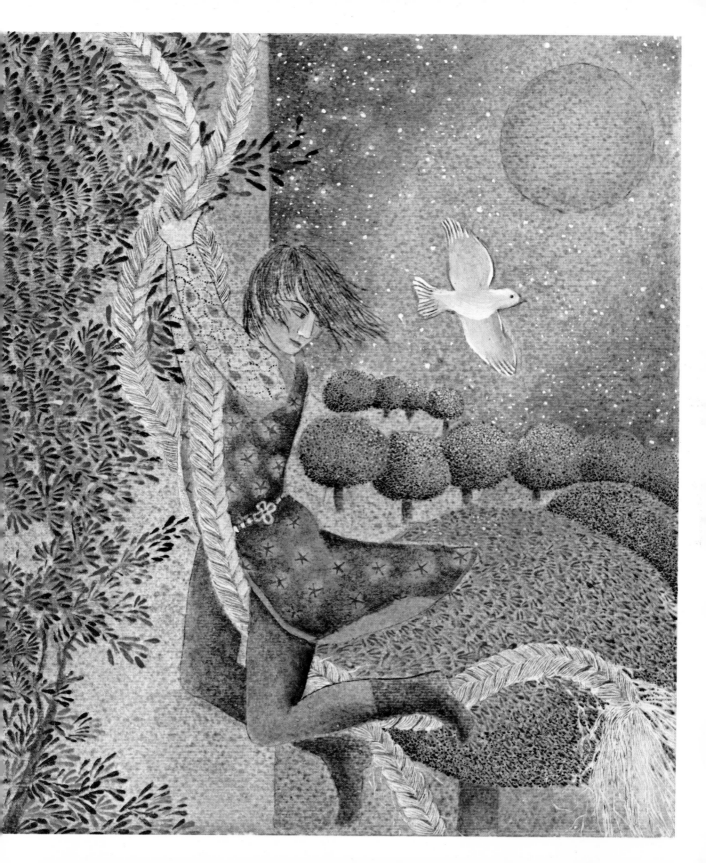

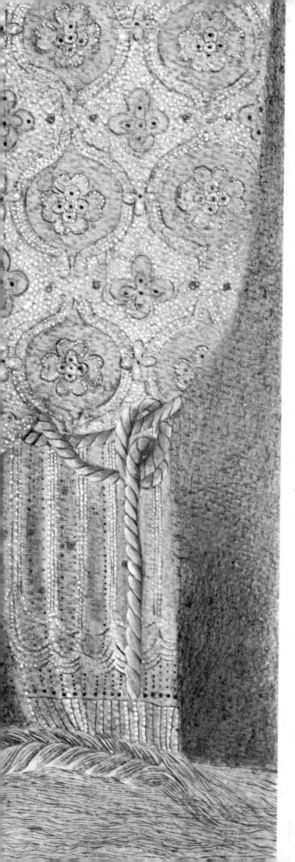

AT first Rapunzel was alarmed when the prince appeared, for she had never seen anyone before but the witch. But he talked to her so kindly that she soon lost her fear. "Your singing brought me here," said the prince. "I listened so often." And he begged her to escape and be his wife.

"I would come gladly," said Rapunzel, "but how can it be done?"

At last they thought of a plan. Every night the prince would bring a skein of silk. Rapunzel would weave this into a ladder; when it was long enough to reach the ground, she would climb down to freedom, and away they would ride together.

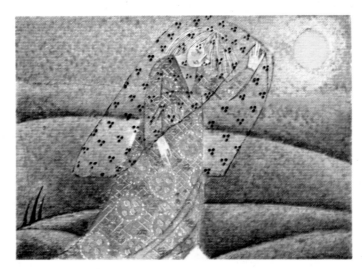

EACH night the silken ladder grew longer; each day Rapunzel
hid it well. But one day she made a dreadful mistake! "Tell me,
Mother," she said. "Why do you climb so slowly up to the
window? The prince is here quick as lightning." Oh—what had
she said! The witch was in a frenzy.

"So you've had a visitor!" she hissed. "I thought I had kept you
from the world, but you have deceived me. Well, there's an answer
to that." She snatched up a pair of scissors, grasped the thick hair
in her other hand, and—snip! snap!—the golden tresses fell and
covered the floor. Then the witch-woman dragged the poor girl off
to a forest wilderness, and left her there to live on berries and nuts
as best she could.

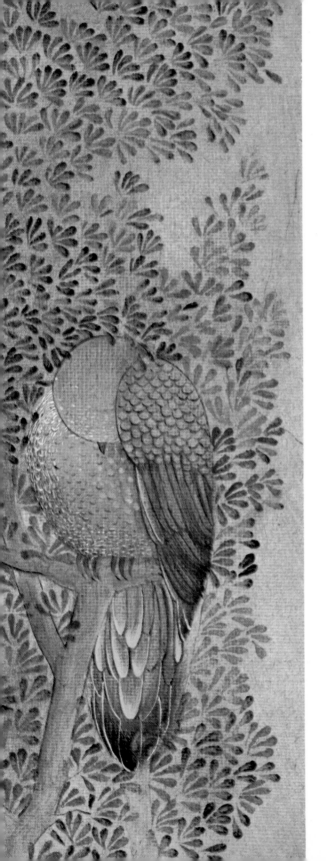

BACK in the tower the witch picked up the severed hair and wound it around a hook. She did not have to wait long. Far down below came the call:

Rapunzel, Rapunzel,
Let down your golden hair!

The golden hair came down; the prince climbed up—but imagine his horror when the window came into view! There he beheld not the lovely Rapunzel but the mocking face of the witch. "Ha!" she cried. "So you've come for my daughter! But you are too late—the bird has flown. You'll never see her again." She burst into peals of laughter—and the prince, maddened by shock and despair, leaped from the window to the ground. Down . . . down. . . .

HE was not killed, for a great bush of thorns broke his fall. But the thorns pierced his eyes and made him blind. Sadly he wandered back and forth through the land, through the forest, thinking only of the beautiful girl who should have become his bride.

MANY months—perhaps even years—had passed when by chance the prince wandered into the wilderness that was now Rapunzel's home. She lived there in utter poverty with the little twins, boy and girl, who had been born to her in the forest. Suddenly he stopped. That voice, that singing—whose could it be but Rapunzel's? He moved toward the sound. Rapunzel saw him and twined her arms around him, tears running down her face. Two of the tears fell on the prince's eyes—wonderful! He could see! So they made their joyful return to his kingdom, where they lived happily ever after.

Copyright © 1982 by Jutta Ash
All rights reserved, including the right to reproduce this book or
portions thereof in any form.
First published in the United States by Holt, Rinehart and Winston,
383 Madison Avenue, New York, New York 10017.

Library of Congress Cataloging in Publication Data
Main entry under title:
Rapunzel.
Summary: A beautiful girl with long golden hair is imprisoned in a
lonely tower by a witch.
[1. Fairy tales. 2. Folklore—Germany] I. Ash,
Jutta, ill. II. Rapunzel. English.
PZ8.R1865 1982   398.2'1'0943 [E]   81-13284
ISBN 0-03-061219-5   AACR2

First American Edition

Printed in Italy
1 3 5 7 9 10 8 6 4 2